Dear Parent:
Your child's love of reading starts here!

Every child learns to read in a different way and at his or her own speed. Some go back and forth between reading levels and read favorite books again and again. Others read through each level in order. You can help your young reader improve and become more confident by encouraging his or her own interests and abilities. From books your child reads with you to the first books he or she reads alone, there are I Can Read Books for every stage of reading:

SHARED READING
Basic language, word repetition, and whimsical illustrations, ideal for sharing with your emergent reader

BEGINNING READING
Short sentences, familiar words, and simple concepts for children eager to read on their own

READING WITH HELP
Engaging stories, longer sentences, and language play for developing readers

READING ALONE
Complex plots, challenging vocabulary, and high-interest topics for the independent reader

ADVANCED READING
Short paragraphs, chapters, and exciting themes for the perfect bridge to chapter books

I Can Read Books have introduced children to the joy of reading since 1957. Featuring award-winning authors and illustrators and a fabulous cast of beloved characters, I Can Read Books set the standard for beginning readers.

A lifetime of discovery begins with the magical words **"I Can Read!"**

Visit www.icanread.com for information
on enriching your child's reading experience.

Dirt on My Shirt

SELECTED POEMS

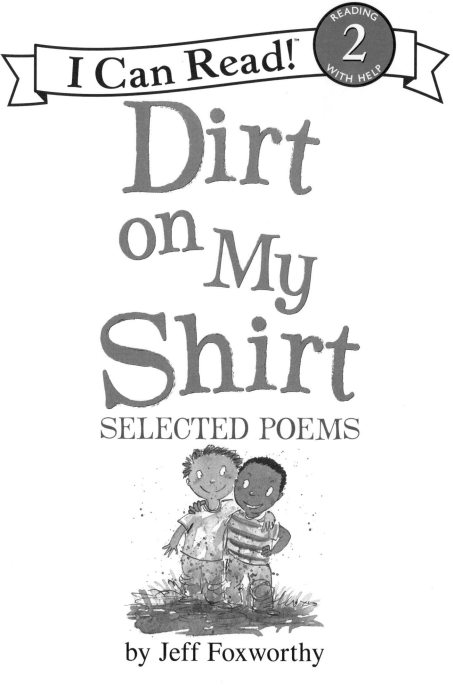

by Jeff Foxworthy

pictures by Steve Björkman

HarperCollins*Publishers*

HarperCollins®, ☎®, and I Can Read Book® are trademarks of HarperCollins Publishers.

Dirt on My Shirt: Selected Poems
Copyright © 2008 by Jeff Foxworthy

Manufactured in China.

For information address HarperCollins Children's Books, a division of HarperCollins Publishers,
10 East 53rd Street, New York, NY 10022.
www.icanread.com

Library of Congress catalog card number: 2008005793
ISBN 978-0-06-176525-4 (trade bdg.) — ISBN 978-0-06-176524-7 (pbk.)

Typography by Rick Farley
09 10 11 12 13 SCP 10 9 8 7 6 5 4 3 2 1
❖
First Edition
Originally published in an unabridged edition by HarperCollins, 2008

For Maggie, ever the encourager and always a friend.
Thank you for nudging me down this path.
—J.F.

To the students at Greentree Elementary
and their dedicated principal, Dianne Ball.
—S.B.

Table of Contents

Dirt on My Shirt

There's dirt on my shirt

And leaves in my hair

There's mud on my boots

But I don't really care

Playing outside is so much fun

To breathe the clean air

And feel the warm sun

To stomp in a puddle

Or climb a big tree

Makes me quite happy

Just look and you'll see

Staring Contest

I am staring at my cat

He doesn't bat an eye

Watching me, watching him

The seconds tick on by

Tears come to my eyes

I'm going to have to blink

He smiles a silly cat smile

And then gives me a wink

Deer

An eye

Then an ear

I think I see a deer

Hiding behind that big tree

A stomp

Then a flash

And he's gone in a dash

I think the deer just saw me

Uninvited Guests

Atop our bird feeder's a squirrel

> we call Peter

Who's eating seeds meant for others

The birds are concerned,

> because they just learned

He's invited his sisters and brothers!

Friends

Friends come in all colors

And sizes and shapes

Friends share their jump ropes

And friends share their grapes

They like the same jokes

And they like the same shows

They lend you their ear

And they lend you their clothes

A world without friends

I don't think I could bear it

Life is much better

With good friends to share it

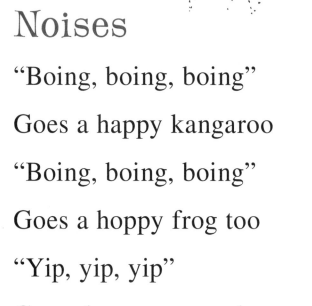

Noises

"Boing, boing, boing"

Goes a happy kangaroo

"Boing, boing, boing"

Goes a hoppy frog too

"Yip, yip, yip"

Goes the puppy up the street

"Tweet, tweet, tweet"

Goes our little parakeet

"Ding-a-ling-a-ling"

Goes a fire truck in a hurry

"Wah, wah, wah"

Goes my baby brother Murray

Missing

I had a tadpole in a bowl

But now he's disappeared

Where he swam a frog now sits

I think that's kinda weird

Are We There Yet?

The Jenkins went out for a ride

"How much longer?" the children cried

"A while!" their dad said with regret

"We haven't left the driveway yet!"

Wishing and Fishing

I was just wishing

That I could go fishing

What I might catch

I don't know

A shark or a whale,

Or a fish with no tail

No matter 'cause I'll let 'em go

Auntie Brooke

My Auntie Brooke just loves to cook

From turkey to cookies to bread

When she makes spaghetti,

You'd better get ready

For meatballs the size of your head!

She once made a cake as big as a lake

A cement truck stirred up the batter

She put on the icing that was so enticing

With the oar from a boat and a ladder

Uncle Moe

My Uncle Moe

Has a big mustache

It's bushy as can be

When he stands up

Straight and tall

He looks just like a tree!

Uncle Keith

My Uncle Keith has great big teeth

He can eat corn really fast

My Grandma Rose has a really big nose

When she sneezes it's more like a blast

Grandma

My grandma puts on lipstick

It's bright red like a rose

Because she cannot see too well

It ends up on her nose!

Granddaddy

It sounds kind of sappy,

  but it makes me happy

To sit in my granddaddy's lap

He tickles,

  I giggles and wiggles like crazy

And sometimes we just like to nap

Sharing a Bed

Sharing a bed with your cousins

Is not the easiest thing

They toss and they turn

They giggle and snore

And sometimes

They just like to sing

Escape

How happy are balloons

That finally get away?

Escaped from little hands

That tried to make them stay

Where do they go, I wonder?

With no map to guide them

To Heaven I would guess

Where little angels ride them